ONE MORE TIME

For Simon and Liz

ONE MORE TIME

LOUIS BAUM
ILLUSTRATED BY
PADDY BOUMA

MULBERRY BOOKS, NEW YORK

Text copyright © 1986 by Louis Baum
Illustrations copyright © 1986 by Paddy Bouma
First Published in Great Britain in 1986 by The Bodley Head, Ltd., 30 Bedford Square, London WC1B 3RP under the
title ARE WE NEARLY THERE?
Library of Congress Catalog Card Number: 85-31050
ISBN 0-688-11698-1

Simon and Dad are sailing their boat in the park on
Sunday afternoon.

The boat goes around and around the sunny pond.

"It's late," says Dad. "It's time to go."

"One more time," says Simon.

"One more time," says Dad.

One more time the boat goes around.
"One more time," says Simon.
"Time to go," says Dad.

Dad gathers boots, coat, bag, boat, book, picnic basket, and stroller.

"All together and ready to go?"

"Ready to go," says Simon.

"Well, let's go then," says Dad.

"Can I have a balloon, Dad? A red one, please?"

"One balloon, a red one, please," says Dad.

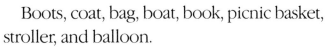

Boots, coat, bag, boat, book, picnic basket,
stroller, and balloon.
 "All together and ready to go?"
 "Ready to go," says Simon.

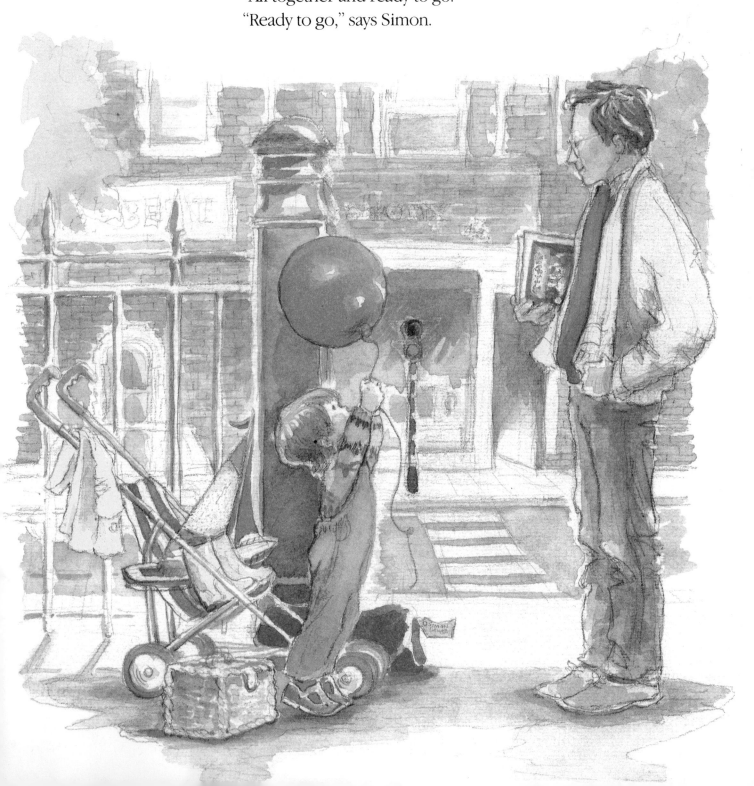

"Return ticket for one, please."
"Can I have a ticket, too, please, Dad?"
"You're still too little to need a ticket."
"Why am I still too little, Dad?"
"Well, you're not really too little. You're getting bigger every day."

The train is waiting on Track Nine.
"Is it going soon?" asks Simon.
"Any minute now," says Dad.

Slowly the train pulls out of the station. Near the track there
are old buildings, empty on Sunday afternoon.
"Are we almost there?" asks Simon.
"We've hardly even started," says Dad.

Now there are houses near the track, each with a little garden
and a little garden shed. And there are clotheslines and people
and chimneys in a row.

"Is it very far?" asks Simon.

"Not very far," says Dad.

Then the countryside begins. There are fields and farms with cows and tractors, and trees and winding country roads. The sun is setting over them through the clouds.

"Are we almost there?" asks Simon.
"Still a little way to go," says Dad.
"It isn't very far, is it, Dad?" asks Simon.
"No, not very far."

"Would you like me to read you a story?"
"I'm hungry," says Simon.
"Then let's have a picnic instead," says Dad.
"Oh, yes, let's have a picnic."

"One more tomato," says Simon.
"No more tomatoes," says Dad.

Trees and tractors and sleepy cows, and the sun going down over a hill.

"Would you like me to read you a story now?" asks Dad.

"Yes, please," says Simon.

"Once upon a time in a distant land, so far away that most people didn't know where it was—"

"Is it very far?" asks Simon.

"Not very far," says Dad.

"Will you read the story one more time,
please?" asks Simon.
"One more time," says Dad.

"Who can see it first?" asks Dad.

"I can see it first!" says Simon.

Behind the hill is a little town. Its lights are beginning to twinkle.

"Are we almost there?" asks Simon.
"Almost there," says Dad.
Slowly the train comes into the station and stops.

"Now for a little walk," says Dad.
"It isn't very far, is it, Dad?" asks Simon.
"Not very far at all," says Dad.
"Are we almost there?" asks Simon.
"Almost there," says Dad.

"Who can see it first?" asks Dad.

"I can see it first!" says Simon.

Around the corner is a dark street and a house with bright lights shining in the windows.

"We're almost there," says Simon.

"Almost there," says Dad.

Dad gathers boots, coat, bag, boat, book, stroller, and balloon.
"All together?"
"All together. Lift me up so I can ring the doorbell, Dad."

"One more time," says Simon.
"Once is enough."

"One more hug," says Simon.
"One more hug," says Dad.

"Hello, Simon."
"Hello, Mom."

"Good-bye, Simon."
"Good-bye, Dad."

"See you soon," says Dad.
"See you soon," says Simon.